Mary Blount Christian

SEBASTIAN (Super Sleuth) and the Egyptian Connection

Illustrated by Lisa McCue

S0-BRW-568

ALADDIN BOOKS
Macmillan Publishing Company   New York
Maxwell Macmillan Canada   Toronto
Maxwell Macmillan International
New York   Oxford   Singapore   Sydney

To Christopher
(Super Reader)

First Aladdin Books edition 1991

Text copyright © 1988 by Mary Blount Christian

Illustrations copyright © 1988 by Lisa McCue

Aladdin Books
Macmillan Publishing Company
866 Third Avenue
New York, NY 10022

Maxwell Macmillan Canada, Inc.
1200 Eglinton Avenue East
Suite 200
Don Mills, Ontario M3C 3N1

Macmillan Publishing Company is part of the Maxwell Communication
Group of Companies.

Printed in the United States of America

A hardcover edition of *Sebastian (Super Sleuth) and the Egyptian Connection*
is available from Macmillan Publishing Company.

1 2 3 4 5 6 7 8 9 10

Library of Congress Cataloging-in-Publication Data

Christian, Mary Blount.
Sebastian (super sleuth) and the Egyptian connection / by Mary
Blount Christian ; illustrated by Lisa McCue. — 1st Aladdin Books ed.
p. cm.
Summary: Dog detective Sebastian helps his master find a shipment
of stolen Egyptian artifacts that is being smuggled into the country.
ISBN 0-689-71514-5 (pbk.)
[1. Dogs—Fiction. 2. Smuggling—Fiction. 3. Mystery and
detective stories.] I. McCue, Lisa, ill. II. Title.
[PZ7.C4528Sdd 1991]
[Fic]—dc20 91-15519 CIP AC

Contents

1
What Does a Nose Know?

Sebastian shot a critical sidelong glance at Lady Sharon, Maude Culpepper's Old English sheepdog. The nerve of that bag of fur, lollygagging on *his* favorite spot on *his* couch! A low rumble escaped his fuzzy lips.

"Sebastian!" John yelled from the kitchen, where he and Maude were painting the cabinets. "Enough of that, now. Be a good host."

John Quincy Jones, Sebastian's human, had Sundays off from his job as a city police detective and had decided to give the kitchen a fresh coat of paint. Sebastian, the unofficial but far superior detective, had the day off, too, although he had no intention of spending it painting.

Maude—John called her his girlfriend—had offered to help, though. That was okay, Sebastian figured, but he hated it when John paid more attention

1

to her than to him! And he especially didn't like it when Maude brought Lady Sharon. There was room for only one dog in John's life—and that was the hairy hawkshaw!

Lady Sharon, asleep on the couch, snorted. *Humpt!* Sebastian pouted. Who did she think she was, anyway? Well, she was no *real* competition. Shrugging off thoughts of her like fleas, Sebastian trotted toward the kitchen. How was the painting going? he wondered. And would he approve of the color? It was time he got a look at it.

What was that ladder doing stretched across the kitchen doorway? Well, if he wiggled a little *this* way, then scooted *that* way, he could just make it through. *Ooof!* It was a tighter squeeze than he'd first thought; his flanks were stuck. Sebastian struggled to free himself. The ladder teetered.

"Look out!" Maude shrieked, reaching out too late to steady the ladder.

John, who unfortunately was *on* the ladder, threw up his arms. *Whop!* Gooey sticky paint—azure blue, as it turned out—plopped all over Sebastian's fur.

"Oh, no! Sebastian!" John yelled, scrambling down the ladder.

"Oh, horrors." Maude groaned.

Sebastian wiggled free of the ladder and shook. Blue paint splattered all over Maude, John, the cabinets, and the newspapers that John had spread on

2

the floor to protect the linoleum. Now Sebastian was really in trouble!

Quickly he slumped into a hangdog position and whimpered pitifully, rolling his eyes. That always got to John. He couldn't fuss at such a winsome canine, could he?

"Stay there on those papers and don't move a muscle!" John commanded. He grabbed a can of turpentine and a couple of rags. John tossed one of the rags to Maude, who dabbed at the paint on the appliances while he tried to clean up Sebastian.

Phew! That stuff smelled awful, and it made Sebastian's eyes water.

"I guess that's about as clean as I can get you," John muttered, just as Sebastian was about to give up hope. "Now, you stay right there on those papers," he told Sebastian.

Turning toward Maude, John asked, "How about some pizza? I've got a couple in the freezer and can pop 'em in the oven real quick."

"Sounds great," Maude told him. "I'll make some coffee. And should I feed the dogs something? Do you have any dry dog food here?" She peeked inside a couple of cabinets as she spoke, retrieving a jar of instant coffee.

"No," John said, "and it's the strangest thing, too. I know I buy it, but I can never find it when I want it."

4

Actually, there was nothing strange about it. John brought it in, and Sebastian dragged it out through the doggie door to the bird feeder. He hoped John would eventually get tired of bringing the yukky stuff home.

"I guess they can have a little of the pizza. It's got meat and cheese and stuff like that," John suggested.

Now he was talking! All that *good* stuff!

While John was baking the pizza and making a tossed green salad for himself and Maude, Sebastian entertained himself by reading the newspapers spread around him. Might as well read; sitting was so boring. Besides, it was the only thing he could do without getting into trouble. *Hmmm*. The Tigers had won another football game, the headline said. Who'd want to name a team after cats, even big ones? There was a story about some city councilman griping about a new sculpture put in front of City Hall. It was pretty silly looking. Sebastian belly-crawled to another page. John had told him to stay still, but surely he hadn't meant for him to read the same page over and over. What was that weird picture?

Cautiously Sebastian leaned forward to get a closer look. It was a house that looked like a pyramid, stuck right in the middle of a neighborhood. The picture showed neighbors marching in front of it with protest signs. "It's un-American," an unidentified neighbor complained. "Why couldn't he build Greek Revival or French Provincial like the rest of us?"

Sebastian read on: "Carmine Rothwi . . . "—there was a blob of blue paint blocking the rest of the name— "has announced he will show off his home, which is decorated throughout with replicas of Egyptian artifacts and household furniture at . . . " That was blotted out with paint, too.

"Pizza's served. You can get up now, Sebastian," John said.

Wiggling with delight, Sebastian hurried to his plate to get his pizza. But what a shock! He couldn't smell it! All he could smell was that turpentine. And since he couldn't smell the pizza, he could barely taste it. Sighing, he ate, anyway, assuring himself that he must be enjoying it. After all, he always had before.

While they were eating, the phone rang. John answered. "Hasan! Hasan, is it really you?" He cupped his hand over the phone and quickly told Maude, "It's Hasan el-Salim, my Egyptian friend."

Sebastian jumped onto the couch and glared at Lady Sharon until she moved over. He'd heard about Hasan before. He was a detective in Alexandria, Egypt, and had trained with John at the police academy. The city often let some of their police train in a foreign country, and that country sent a few of its own police to train in the city. That way they could learn each other's methods of detection and maybe pick up new ideas to take home.

John and Hasan had become the best of friends. That was before Sebastian and John had met, of course.

"We'll meet you there. See you then!" John hung up, excited. "It'll be wonderful to see Hasan again. He's coming on a case, but he didn't want to discuss it over the phone. He's going to ask Chief for my help," he told Maude. Chief was John's (and, indirectly, Sebastian's) boss, a beetle-browed grouch of a man.

John was forgetting all about *him* again. What help could John be without his fuzzy partner?

But, wait a minute! What about his sense of smell? That pizza might as well have been crushed concrete, for all he could tell. How would he manage to sniff out clues?

2
A Glimmer of Hope

Sebastian awoke the next morning to the sound of sizzling bacon and eggs. But he could barely smell them. And his nose felt tender, too. Disappointing. But then, if he had a little sense of smell back now, surely the rest would return soon. He trotted into the kitchen, carefully avoiding the new paint. He didn't want to get turpentined again!

John was whistling under his breath. He seemed really happy this morning. Sebastian remembered that it was because of Hasan.

While Sebastian ate his own breakfast of chopped beef, cheese, and eggs, John called Chief. "I'll be a little late this morning, Chief. I'm supposed to pick up Detective el-Salim at the airport. You remember Hasan from academy days, don't you, Chief? He did talk to you from the airplane first thing this morning, didn't he?"

John paused, listening, then said, "Chief, he didn't ask for me to be assigned to the case with him just because we're friends. . . . No, sir, I'm *not* going to be in the way." John hung up and made a face. "Why can't Chief give me any credit?" he muttered.

Sebastian knew exactly how John felt! *He* didn't get any credit, either. And if there was anyone Chief liked less than John, it was Sebastian.

It was around ten in the morning when John and Sebastian went to the airport. The big Egypt Air plane was just landing.

By the time John had found a parking space, Hasan was emerging from the customs area with his luggage. John rushed to embrace the slender, dark-eyed man with the wide smile.

"John, my friend, time has been good to you," Hasan said. He pulled back and looked at Sebastian. "Ah, and this must be the fine animal you described in your letters. Sebastian, you said?"

John had written Hasan about him? He must have been quite complimentary, from what Hasan said. The cuddly canine blushed right through the fuzz on his face.

Hasan offered his hand, palm up, in a gesture of goodwill. Sebastian nuzzled it. Then Hasan scratched Sebastian behind the ears and became an instant friend.

Sebastian trotted alongside Hasan and John, eavesdropping.

"So, what's this case all about, Hasan?" John

asked as they strolled toward the car. "I can't imagine what sort of case would bring you all the way to our part of the world, unless, of course, you're working on a smuggling case."

"Ah, my friend, John, as sharp as ever," Hasan said.

Sebastian sniffed indignantly. He'd been just about to guess that himself.

John, Hasan, and Sebastian went straight to Chief's office. Chief leaned across his desk to shake hands with Hasan, glare at John, and snarl at Sebastian. "Welcome back to America, Detective el-Salim. John, why are *you* here? Don't you dare eat my diet salad, you four-legged garbage disposal."

Hasan smiled at Chief as he spoke. "I have asked my friend John to work with me—with your permission, naturally. We work together so well, you understand."

Chief walked around to the front of his desk. "Hmmm, yes, certainly—if you don't think he and that fleabag will get in the way. So tell me why you are here, Detective el-Salim." He motioned for them to sit down.

Sebastian broke into a panting grin and slid closer to Chief's "diet" salad. He may not have had all of his sense of smell back, but he could see calorie-dripping dressing, fat chunks of cheese, and strips of juicy ham. Not very dietetic, actually. He inhaled the aromas, which were now only slightly tainted with turpentine.

"I am in search of smugglers who have taken some of our national treasures." Hasan pulled photos from a file folder and spread them over the desk. "Priceless treasures from the tomb of Snoferu."

"Snoferu?" Chief said. "I thought his name was Toot or Tuf or—"

"Tutankhamen?" Hasan said. "Egypt had many kings in its history. Snoferu is not as well known as the boy king, of course. But his treasures belong to Egypt, all the same, and they are just as rare and precious."

Fourth dynasty, wasn't it? Sebastian wondered, searching his keen mind. He'd read all about that. Yes, first king of the fourth, he recalled.

"Snoferu was the first king of the fourth dynasty," Hasan said, confirming the hairy hawkshaw's memory. "Look for yourselves at these photographs. They reveal the exquisite craftsmanship of a past life— irreplaceable sculptures and artifacts."

Sebastian stretched his neck to see. There were lots of pretty pieces made of gold and turquoise and shiny white or black rocklike stuff. *Ikk!* One piece was a black cat with eyes of green-colored glass and a turquoise collar. Poor ancient Egyptians: They had no Old English sheepdogs to brighten their lives. But cats? Really! Sebastian squinted at the typed

description under the picture. It said the statue was made of onyx, which must be that black stuff. The white stuff, then, must be the alabaster the description mentioned. He did regret he hadn't studied geology more. He made a mental note to correct that next time John went to the library.

Some of the pieces were solid gold. One was a ceremonial mummy mask with colored glass designs on it; another was a statue of a cobra with its hood spread out. There were other gold pieces, too: rings, bracelets, carved cups, and boxes.

Hasan pointed to the photo of a running deer carved from ivory and painted gold. "This is a whip handle," he said. "And this lion's head is from a solid-gold bed," he told them.

Beautiful, Sebastian thought. As beautiful as a dog's cold nose on a summer's day. They belonged to the world, not some miserly old thief. He had to find them and help Hasan return them to Egypt.

"These priceless pieces were in the basement of our museum in Cairo waiting to be cataloged and prepared for display, when they were stolen. I managed to track the thieves and the artifacts to a warehouse in Alexandria. But, alas, I was alone. I was able to handcuff two of them to metal posts, but I was then overwhelmed by the other two. They not only avoided capture, but also left the two handcuffed thieves behind, demonstrating their poor character. They got away with the—how do you say?—goods. It was two days before my men found us there," Hasan said.

Alexandria, Egypt, Sebastian recalled, had a shipping port, as well as airports. And, of course, it had postal services, too.

"By the time I was released from the hospital and able to obtain the necessary papers and funds to come here in pursuit, they had gotten five more days' head start on me. If they used a cargo plane to bring in the artifacts, they may have beaten me here," Hasan said.

"Naturally we questioned the captured men at length. Their testimonies seemed to agree that *your* city is to be the recipient of the artifacts," Hasan told John and Chief. He brightened. "And I have reason to believe they are bringing the artifacts by sea. One of those who got away had a tattoo on his arm; it was of a ship. I think he is a sailor. Besides, one of his captured cohorts practically admitted this."

Sebastian nodded admiringly. Hasan had noticed the ship tattoo—not bad detective work.

Hasan cupped his head in his hands. "I let these beautiful treasures from our past slip through my fingers. I have failed my country miserably. I must find them. I must."

Sebastian ached for Hasan. While he, himself,

14

had never failed in a task, he could imagine how horrible it would feel.

Hasan pressed his lips together and narrowed his gaze before speaking again. "During the struggle with the thieves, my gun fired accidentally, and I hit several of the packing cases. I feel certain that the spent bullets lodged in the thick packing material surrounding the stolen pieces. The thieves did not examine the cases after I was tied up, and if they did not repackage the pieces . . ."

John leaped to his feet. "We'll alert the port customs inspectors immediately. They have several teams of dogs trained in sniffing out gunpowder. We'll notify the airport and postal securities, too, just in case that tattoo meant nothing."

Good work. John was covering all the angles, just as the old hairy hawkshaw would. But they shouldn't depend on those strange dogs! A sensitive nose was a gift! Those dogs were taught to respond to just one odor, and they were trained like a bunch of senseless puppies at that! The trainer would soak their toys in the odor, then allow them to play only when they had detected that odor hidden away!

Most of the dogs were trained to smell a specific drug or perhaps plastique explosive or gunpowder. But because of illegal-weapons exporting, officers were now training some dogs to react to the smell of the packing grease used to coat the weapons during transport. Generally, the dogs worked in teams—one an expert in gunpowder and the other a specialist in packing grease. They checked outgoing cases, while a team of drug-sniffing dogs worked the incoming material.

Now, he, Sebastian (Super Sleuth), had the ability to distinguish a full range of smells, and not from playing silly games, either. It was a natural ability, for which he was grateful to his mother and father.

Sebastian moved closer to Chief's salad and sucked up the strips of ham. *Ummm.* He slurped up the cheese. Only the hairy hawkshaw could detect the difference between fine mozzarella cheese and Monterey jack—until the terrible turpentine incident, that is.

"Then it's settled, Detective el-Salim," Chief said. "We'll alert the customs folks right away. You will have at your disposal any of our men and dogs. Are you sure you don't want some *other* detective? Hey! That walking garbage can ate my diet salad!"

Sebastian licked his lips. Correction, Chief. The "diet" part, the lettuce, was still intact. He'd actually done Chief a favor, getting all that fat stuff out! The cagey canine trotted out the door ahead of John and Hasan, eager to get away from Chief's nasty glare.

But mostly he was anxious to get to work on the case. Smugglers, beware, for Sebastian (Super Sleuth) was on the job now!

3
Scent-illating Crime

As they hurried from the police station, Sebastian stuck close to Hasan, listening to everything he had to say. The hairy hawkshaw's keen ears and eyes, his superintelligence—these would serve him well until his nose regained its full abilities.

"Do you think someone will ask for ransom?" John asked, voicing a question that was racing through Sebastian's mind, too. These thieves might figure the Egyptian government would be willing to pay lots of money for the return of the artifacts.

"We have not ruled that out, of course. But we think otherwise," Hasan replied. "Had they wished just to hide the items away, the hills are dotted with caves. They would not have had to chance being caught while transporting the pieces."

"What if they melted the pieces down?" John said. "We'd never find them."

Hasan shook his head. "Gold is still valuable. But turquoise is common, as are glass and stones. The pieces are valuable for what they are—ancient relics, an artistry gone forever."

"But what else could anyone do with them?" John blurted out. Sebastian was so proud of him. He was asking all the right questions.

"You would be surprised, my friend, at the number of museums in the world that are displaying ill-gotten pieces of our past. And then, there might be very rich private collectors who enjoy having rare bits of history around them."

"But what's the use of having artifacts if you can't show them off?" John wanted to know.

Hasan shrugged. "Perhaps displaying the artifacts isn't as important to these possibly eccentric persons as owning them. Or perhaps they like the excitement of knowing that tucked away in some dark vault are pieces coveted by many, pieces that are priceless and unique. Maybe they will stay hidden for many years until, as you say, the heat is off."

Sebastian's mouth watered. That made sense. He could understand the excitement of having something tucked away, something coveted by others. Think of all those lovely bones he had buried around the yard. It was exciting to know that they were hidden, and that plenty of dogs—including Lady Sharon—would love to get their paws on them. But why want something you couldn't chew or eat or sleep in?

"We believe that the smuggler must be a private collector who has hired thieves to steal the pieces," Hasan said. "I am afraid that once the artifacts reach that person, they will be lost. Therefore it is most important that we find them at the port, before the thieves can deliver the stolen pieces."

Sebastian sighed wearily. The port was a big place. Ships were stacked up in the channel, waiting to get a berth on the dock and be unloaded and reloaded. Fishermen and shrimpers had to weave their way through all the ships just to bring their catches in for sale. And how would the pieces be packed? Hasan had said in boxes with protective insulation. He hadn't mentioned any labels on the boxes, however.

"Hasan, were the boxes that you hit with your bullets marked in any way?" John asked, once more voicing Sebastian's own thoughts.

"There were no marks," Hasan said. "They could be labeled by now, however. The boxes might say anything. They might even have been exchanged for other boxes. In that case, we are lost, we are lost." Hasan sounded frantic, and his face seemed to wilt.

"Now, don't worry, Hasan," John told him. "We're on the case together now."

Was John finally giving Sebastian the credit he so deserved?

"Yessir, Hasan, with you and me working together the way we did in the police academy, nobody's getting away with this!" John finished.

Humpt! Sebastian mulled over what he knew. The pieces would be heavy, very heavy. And they could come labeled as anything from tools to straw hats, and in boxes of a variety of sizes. They might even have been hidden away in the trunk of a car. Or shipped in the bowels of an oil tanker. How could the police check every single box in every single ship coming in from Egypt? It seemed an impossible task.

"I'm going to drop Sebastian off at the house," John told Hasan when they reached the car. "I hate to leave him at home, since he gets into so much trouble without supervision. But he'd just be in the way at the port. I don't want him getting into any scuffles with the customs dogs."

Trouble? What trouble? Was John still miffed because he'd chewed the corner off the welcome mat? If *that* bothered John, maybe he shouldn't have dropped the jar of barbecue sauce on the mat when he was carrying in the groceries.

What a rotten trick, taking him home. But getting away from home would be as easy as barking. Nobody kept this crime hound out of the action!

4
A Nose for News

Sebastian whimpered woefully as John shoved him into the house. He didn't want John to think he approved of being dumped just as the case got hot.

"Here," John said, hurriedly shoving a milk bone toward Sebastian. "Have a yummy bone. That should make up for being left behind."

Humpt! Not even a real bone. Still, he *was* hungry. He snapped the bone and chomped, swallowing it before the lock on the door clicked.

Sebastian ran to the window and rose up on his hind legs. He pressed his nose to the window and watched. As soon as John's brown car had disappeared around the corner, he dashed through the doggie door and down the sidewalk.

John and Hasan would have the port covered for now. And Hasan was familiar with the stolen relics. Sebastian, on the other hand, had no idea as to the actual sizes of those statues and jars. Then Sebastian remembered the newspaper article about the man who had built himself a pyramid with replicas of Egyptian artifacts and furnishings. Maybe if he got a close look at those fakes he'd have a better idea of what he was looking for. But the paint had obscured part of the owner's name.

Maybe if he slipped into the newspaper office he could find a copy of the story without blue paint. Sebastian trotted to Polk and Travis, where the *City Clarion* building was located. He waited outside until a woman with a camera rushed into the building, and then he went in, too.

Ah, luck was with the old hairy hawkshaw. He saw an open closet behind the receptionist's desk. Since she was too busy reading the comics to notice him, he crept inside and found he had his pick of hats and coats. He wiggled into a trench coat and a battered old felt hat with a pencil and a card in its band that said PRESS PASS.

The receptionist glanced up and nodded at Sebastian as he headed through the swinging door and into the newsroom. Word processors made little clicking noises while reporters hovered over them, typing. A couple of reporters were yelling into phones. They were all too busy to notice a stranger in their midst.

Sebastian spotted the library. Many years ago he'd read somewhere that it was called the morgue. Whatever it was called, that would be where he'd find the story.

The paper John had had on the floor was at least

22

a week old. Sebastian had little hope of finding an old copy of the paper lying around. But he'd done research with John before. He remembered that the newspaper didn't keep clippings of stories anymore. Instead it stored all the stories in computer files.

In the library Sebastian saw several computers lined up against a wall. A huge poster on the wall said: TO USE YOUR LIBRARY COMPUTERS STRIKE GOTO KEY THEN TYPE IN KEY WORDS. That seemed easy enough. But the keys were so little, and his paws were so big! How could he work that machine?

The keen canine mind was never at a loss for long! Sebastian clutched a pencil between his teeth and tapped out the message: GOTO PYRAMIDS. The screen said: ANCIENT OR MODERN? Sebastian moved the cursor to MODERN, then struck EXECUTE.

Sebastian couldn't imagine two men building themselves pyramid houses, but the machine brought up two stories. He dismissed the first one, since that family was in another city. Ah, there it was, the whole story without paint blobs: Mr. Carmine Rothwinger had decided to open his house to the public to "satisfy its curiosity," he said. Then he'd close it forever to public view.

The story went on to say that he was very wealthy and owned several businesses. In his pyramidlike house, he had copies of many of the chairs, tables, and statues found in the tomb of King Tut and other

pharaohs. There was a picture of Mr. Rothwinger holding a walking staff, sort of a long cane, with the image of King Tut carved on its handle. His fingers were covered with rings, some of them not unlike those Sebastian had seen in Hasan's photos. He said the originals were gold, but his were brass. "I love everything ancient Egyptian," he said.

The free open house would be May first. Sebastian glanced at the calendar on the wall. That was today!

He dashed from the library, through the newsroom, and out the door. What a perfect opportunity to get into the house and examine Mr. Rothwinger's pieces. That way the cunning canine would have a more accurate idea of the size of the real ones.

The story had said the house was on Buttercup Lane, and that you couldn't miss it. How right it was! Everywhere on Buttercup Lane, cars were honking and creeping along as passengers hung out their windows and gawked at the weird place. Pedestrians were lined up around the block, shuffling along the sidewalk and through the gate. There it was—a pyramid, right before his eyes.

Sebastian didn't want to get at the end of the line. Detectives hardly had time to waste. Maybe he could slip through. He slumped under the trench coat and hat and crawled along the wall.

"Hey, you!" a man in a security uniform yelled.

Sebastian cringed. Had they found him out?

5
To See the Sea

Sebastian held his breath, awaiting the moment when the man would rip off his press clothes and reveal his true identity. But the guard smiled at him and waved him through. "Reporters don't have to wait," the man said. "Mr. Rothwinger wants all the reporters he can get. Go on in."

Sebastian nodded gratefully as he sauntered past the crowd and through the front door, which oddly enough looked fairly normal. Inside, the rooms didn't look too weird, either, except that the walls leaned in. Everywhere were relics like those he'd seen in Hasan's photos: animal statues, jars, vases, some life-size statues of people, a chair that looked like a throne, and, in the bedroom, a bed with a lion's head on each corner. The bed must be a replica of the one Hasan had said was stolen.

Mr. Rothwinger was prancing around in a gold lamé outfit that looked fit for an Egyptian king. He was waving his hands around so that the rings on his fingers caught the light. Fakes, definitely fakes.

"The alabaster items are really plaster of paris," Mr. Rothwinger said, turning a spread-winged bird upside down to show its chalky bottom. "And the gold-looking things are brass, not even gold plate. The ebony is just painted that way. And the glass beads are machine made. I'm afraid I'm just a big fake!" He chuckled so that his stomach rolled. "I love *everything* Egyptian." He seemed proud of all his phony stuff.

A man in a gray pin-striped suit backed into Sebastian. Instead of apologizing he sneered, crossing his arms across his chest.

"Ah, do I recognize Goodson Wittman, the prominent curator of the fine arts museum?" Mr. Rothwinger gushed. He rushed over, offering a be-ringed hand to the man.

Goodson Wittman didn't take his hand. "I just had to see for myself, Rothwinger. Unbelievable. Simply unbelievable."

"Yes, yes, you like it," he said, nodding.

"I didn't say that! I only said it was unbelievable," Wittman said. "How do you live in this uncomfortable place?"

"Like the pharaohs, dear Wittman," Rothwinger

said. "Like the pharaohs. But, of course, you have many fine Egyptian pieces in your museum." Rothwinger raised his voice slightly. "Not all of it there, shall we say, ummm, legally, ummm?"

Wittman squared his shoulders and jammed his hands into the pockets of his coat. "Almost all museums have such pieces, Rothwinger! We are actually doing countries a favor, preserving their history for them in constant temperatures and favorable light. We—"

Rothwinger glanced around the room as if making sure he had everyone's attention. "Ah, yes. The kindly curator, stealing for the good of others."

Goodson Wittman's face was red, and his eyes seemed to pop from his face. "I do not steal, Rothwinger! I have accepted, er, questionable property, and I'd do it again if I could. We give people the opportunity to see *real* artifacts, not cheap imitations like—"

Rothwinger clasped his hands together. "Yes, yes. They are cheap, and they are imitations. I bow to your expert opinion."

Sebastian was shocked! Why, the man was nothing better than a thief! And he said he'd do it again. Had *he* stolen Hasan's treasures?

A man in white gloves and a suit with tails came in, and Mr. Rothwinger bent to let the man whisper in his ear. He went pale momentarily, but seemed to straighten up. "Gentlemen, gentlemen, do come in. The police, you say?"

It was John and Hasan! They must have had the same idea as he about looking at the replicas. Sebastian jumped, knocking a bowl resembling a lotus cup from a pedestal. It crumbled into powdery chips of plaster of paris. He stood frozen next to the debris, waiting for Rothwinger to yell at him.

Instead, Mr. Rothwinger just laughed. "Not to worry." He dismissed it with a wave of his be-ringed fingers. "As I said, it's merely a cheap copy. There are more where that came from. Don't want to make the press mad. Do you have everything you need?"

Sebastian moved away, trying to keep his back to John and Hasan. What if they recognized him in spite of his disguise? John never had, of course, but what if he *did* someday? He'd be awfully angry! Mr. Rothwinger hadn't yelled at him, but John would!

He scooted past the guards and into the street, hurrying back to the newspaper office to leave the hat and coat before they were missed.

And just in time, too! No sooner had he returned the clothing to the closet and started out than a man with a mustache reached for the hat and coat. "Hey!" he yelled at the receptionist. "How'd my hat get dog fur in it? It was just hanging there in the closet. And look at my coat!"

She rolled her eyes. "Well, everybody says you go

after news like a dog after a fox!" Her shoulders shook as she sniggered.

Sebastian's lips parted in a panting laugh. But enough of this levity. There were smugglers at large! With a better idea about the size of the pieces, he felt it was time to look through the dock area.

Sebastian trotted along the row of warehouses that lined the docks. Fat little fishing trawlers bobbed up and down in the waves, bumping against the dock. Big ships were moored alongside the dock, where handpainted numbers announced their assigned spaces. A conveyer belt was pushed against one, and huge boxes marked FRAGILE/BANANAS were being lowered to the dock from an opening in the side of the ship.

Sebastian's knowledge of the shipping industry wasn't extensive, unfortunately. He figured it would be a good idea to watch for a while.

Each ship he saw had its own name and the name of its owner painted on the bow, he noted. Too bad the print didn't tell where it was coming from, too!

Longshoremen were grabbing the boxes with big hooks and heaving them into trucks. A man stood close by, pointing at one box, then another. The boxes were opened, and the man poked at the banana clusters inside, then waved them away.

Edging closer, Sebastian saw that the man wore a badge that said HEALTH INSPECTOR. There were no dogs sniffing those boxes. And the man looked inside only one out of every hundred or so. How alarming! Why, anything could be in the other boxes.

He crept close to one of the boxes and inhaled deeply. There was a strong banana scent. At last his sense of smell seemed completely intact. Now that he was closer, Sebastian could see smaller print on the boxes. It said Honduras. Wasn't that in Central America? No danger of the artifacts being in one of those packages. But what if the inspectors checked only a few boxes shipped from Alexandria? The artifacts could slip right through their—

"Hey!" a man with hairy arms and big ears yelled. "Get away from there, you mangy mutt!" A hook sailed past Sebastian's left ear and stuck in one of the boxes. "Somebody call the dogcatcher!"

Yipping, Sebastian dashed among the forest of legs and down the dock, leaping onto the deck of a fishing trawler. He could hide among the many ice chests on board until the man quit looking for him. *Phew!* This place certainly smelled fishy.

Sebastian crouched there for what must have been five minutes. And all the while, sea gulls, attracted by the smell of the fish, circled overhead, screaming and diving dangerously close to his fuzzy body. *Shoo!*

One ear cocked, he listened. Footsteps were com-

ing! He tensed his muscles, ready to run. A man with a sunburned, weatherbeaten face reached over and heaved one ice chest to his shoulder. His eyes widened. "Hello, poochie. You want to be an old sea dog, maybe?" He laughed as he stepped off the boat and put the chest on the dock.

He stepped back on deck and heaved another chest to his shoulder. "Maybe you better go before the captain sees you, poochie. We gotta sell our fish and shrimp while it's fresh, you know," he told Sebastian. "Here he comes now with some buyers. Run on."

Gratefully, Sebastian scooted off the boat and past the captain and some other people. They were probably restaurant people. That seafood would be on customers' platters tonight.

And speaking of tonight, he had better get home before John did.

As he trotted home, he thought about the artifacts. It had been two days before Hasan was found by his men. He had been in the hospital another day. Then it had taken two days for Hasan's travel request to be reviewed and approved by his superiors, and another two days before he had gotten the money from his department accountant.

If the artifacts were coming by ship, and the ship made stops along the way, it could be a month before they arrived in port. But if the ship was fast and had no delays, Sebastian figured the artifacts would arrive tomorrow at the earliest. Maybe he could find out if any ships were coming from Alexandria in the next few days. The next day's arrivals and departures of ships were always in the newspaper on the business pages. He could check there before dinner. On second thought, *after* dinner. He was starving!

Sebastian had just dashed through the doggie door and settled himself on the couch when John got home.

John walked through all the rooms, then returned, smiling. "Good dog! I can't find anything broken or torn. What a good dog you've been! Come, boy. Hasan is in the car, waiting. We're having dinner at Maude's. Come!"

Maude met them at the door. "I hope you all like fish!" she said. "I've fixed blackened redfish, boiled potatoes, and slaw."

Fish? *Ikk!* After smelling the port today, he was not all that enthusiastic about fish. It may have been Sebastian's imagination, but he thought he saw a flicker of the same feeling on the faces of John and Hasan.

"Any luck on your case?" Maude asked as she set the table.

"Not really," John said. "We're checking all of the ships coming from the Middle East or from connections with ships from the Middle East. Maybe something will turn up."

"Yes," Hasan said, sighing wistfully, "we are not overlooking the possibility that the artifacts might have changed ships. So many ships to check, it is like your saying about looking for a needle in a haystack."

Sebastian echoed Hasan's sigh. Detective work was like that. You had to turn over a lot of hay before you found the needle. And you had to examine a lot of clues before you found the solution.

Maude invited them to sit down at the table. "I've picked the bones out of some redfish for the dogs to eat, so let's dig in."

While they ate—the humans at the table, and Sebastian and Lady Sharon on the floor in the kitchen—Sebastian reviewed the clues:

Most of the Egyptian artifacts stolen from the Cairo museum basement were small enough to be concealed in cases about the size of bread boxes. The arrested thieves had indicated that the pieces were bound for this city. But what was their final destination? Hasan had said some museums would take stolen artifacts. That Goodson Wittman from the art museum seemed a likely suspect. He had said he would take stolen artifacts, if he could get them! Or the artifacts might be going to a private, eccentric collector. Rothwinger was a collector, and he certainly could be called eccentric. But he was satisfied with replicas.

Ransom seemed an unlikely motive. No one had contacted the Egyptian museum. And, as Hasan said, if the thief wanted ransom, he wouldn't bring the pieces here.

Sebastian slurped the last of his fish, and since Lady Sharon had abandoned a bit on her plate, he ate that, too. He was doing her a favor; fish couldn't be saved.

The humans had eaten and cleared the table, and they were talking in the living room, laughing about John and Hasan's days at the police academy.

Sebastian was free to snoop for the morning newspaper. He found it folded in a basket. He nosed and pawed at it, finally opening it to the shipping news.

The chart said DEP and ARR—that must mean departures and arrivals. He wasn't interested in what was going out, only in what was coming in. It said ARR: 12n/frm: AlexE/Cleopatra/CarmLn/olives/olive oil/dates/B42. That must mean arrival at twelve noon. AlexE had to mean Alexandria, Egypt. And probably the ship's name was *Cleopatra*, and it would be carrying olives, olive oil, and dates. B42—that must be Berth 42. But what did CarmLn mean?

There was a second listing that caught Sebastian's eye: ARR: 3p/frm: AlexE/Bastet/CarmLn/dates/souv'rs/B38. That must mean arrival at three P.M. from Alexandria, Egypt, a ship called *Bastet*—Sebastian curled his lip at that. Wasn't Bastet the Egyptian cat goddess? How could anybody name a ship after a cat? *Ikk!* It was carrying dates and souv'rs—could that be souvenirs? A perfect cover for the real thing! And the berth would be 38.

But there was CarmLn again. What was that? His keen eyes scanned the page until he spotted a key to abbreviations. CarmLn—Carmine Ship Lines. Carmine. . . . Wasn't Mr. Rothwinger's name Carmine? The news article had said he had several businesses. And he himself had said he loved everything Egyptian. Was that why two of his ships were coming from Egypt? Were they bringing him more phony artifacts? Or might the *real* artifacts be aboard? What a perfect setup!

Now to let John know, so he wouldn't have to be watching the entire dock. He grabbed the newspaper to take to John. But that silly Lady Sharon thought he was playing! She grabbed the other end of the paper and tugged with all her might. Sebastian tugged back, growling. This was no time to be a gentleman.

Unfortunately, it only encouraged Lady Sharon to continue her silly game. She growled deep in her throat and held on tightly. Sebastian weighed more, and he was the stronger of the two. So he simply pulled her along with him as he made his way to John and Hasan.

Lady Sharon would have none of this. When Sebastian had almost reached John, she braced herself and yanked hard. *Rrrrrpt!* The paper tore, and Sebastian found himself holding the wrong half.

"Sebastian!" John yelled, grabbing for the ruff around his neck. "No!"

Groaning, Sebastian wiggled free of John's grasp, dropping the piece of paper he held to snap at the one Lady Sharon clutched between her teeth. *Rrrrrpt!* It tore again.

"Naughty!" John yelled, grabbing the paper from Sebastian and at the same time snatching the piece from Lady Sharon. He wadded up the papers and hurried into the kitchen. Sebastian heard the sickening sound of the heavy lid of Maude's kitchen garbage pail clanging shut.

So much for Plan A. He'd just have to go to Plan B. Whatever *that* was.

6
For Two Scents

Sebastian's mind raced while John was driving Hasan to the hotel, then driving home. He finally decided he'd just have to solve the case by himself. So what else was new?

Fortunately, the two ships would dock at widely spaced times. And they would be only four berths apart. That would give him the opportunity to examine the contents of both.

But he would need a disguise. What should he be? A sailor? That would enable him to board the ships and prowl unnoticed among the holds and corridors. Remembering the way the fishing trawler had bobbed up and down and the way those frantic birds kept diving and screaming, he gulped uneasily. Was going aboard really necessary?

"Come along, Sebastian," John interrupted. "Into the house and to bed with you. I really must say that I was disappointed in you tonight, fighting with Lady Sharon over a newspaper, littering Maude's living room with scrap paper. Now, not another peep out of you, old fellow."

Sebastian tucked the stub of his tail close to his body and slunk into the house, trying to look hangdog.

He crept onto the couch and curled himself into a tight ball. He watched John out of the corner of his eye.

"That's better," John said. "Good-night, boy." He turned the light out.

Sebastian's head popped up, and he peered over the couch arm. The bedroom door was shut. Good, John was out of the way. Now the old super sleuth could think things through uninterrupted. The sailor disguise was unappealing, although he would use it in an emergency. Perhaps he could disguise himself as a longshoreman. In overalls, with maybe a knit cap pulled low to conceal his fuzzy ears, he could easily fool anyone around. That wouldn't get him farther than the ship's deck, but it would give him access to the boxes.

Sebastian couldn't remember exactly when the fantastic brain finally shut off for the night, but he slept undisturbed until John woke him up by whistling in the shower.

Sebastian ate his breakfast: tuna, chicken, and cheese with egg. It was not as satisfying as a hamburger, but it would keep the terrific body nourished for the job at hand. As soon as he'd finished eating, a blueberry tart popped out of the toaster. Sebastian rounded out his breakfast with that.

John came into the kitchen and stopped to stare at the toaster. "Hmmm, I thought I put a tart in before I showered. I must be getting absentminded. Oh, well, you finished your breakfast, huh, fellow. Sorry, old man, but I'm going to have to leave you home again. I just don't want you mixing with any customs dogs on the docks. They'll be out in full force today, I'm sure."

Sebastian rolled his eyes and whimpered, turning his head to hide the panting grin that spread across his face. Just as he wanted it—no humans to get in his way.

He counted to twenty after he heard the car leave, then pushed through the doggie door and out into the bright sunshine. What a lovely day to catch a smuggler!

He trotted eagerly toward the port. He loped across the high bridge that crossed the channel. A cargo ship, its deck loaded with rail cars, passed under him, heading out to sea. And a fishing trawler, already low in the water from its catch, was coming in. Sea gulls screamed and dove toward its deck, which was strewn with ice chests. Sebastian's nostrils quivered as he inhaled the strong fish smell. Ah, his nose was working perfectly today.

At the docks, he checked a wall map and found that even-numbered berths were on this side of the channel and odd-numbered berths on the other. So far, so good. He slipped into a warehouse and found a pair of overalls hanging on a nail. A knit cap lay on a bench nearby. Quickly he wiggled into them. He spotted a hook stuck in a bale of hay by the door. Snatching that in his teeth, he trotted outside. He discovered he was now at Berth 30, six berths away from where the *Cleopatra* would dock, four away from where the *Bastet* would berth later.

When he reached Berth 38, a ship was preparing for departure. According to the print on its side, it was called *Thutmos I*. It was being loaded with big boxes stamped MEDICAL SUPPLIES. The customs dogs strolled up and down the stacks of boxes, sniffing. They were probably sniffing for illegal exports of weapons to countries that weren't supposed to get them.

Sebastian sniffed, too. He sniffed again. He knew that smell, and it wasn't medicine. It was oil, like the oil that John used to clean his weapon before department inspections.

How could these dogs miss it? At least one of them was trained to sniff out packing grease for weapons. Yet the dogs trotted right by as if they suspected nothing.

He had to let the customs men know. He rose on

his hind legs and threw his body against the box on top. Off it slid. The crate split open. Out spilled medical supplies.

"Hey!" one of the customs inspectors yelled. He pulled back on his dog's leash and ran over to the box.

Sebastian swallowed hard. How could he have been so wrong? Was his nose ruined forever?

The customs man tried to pick up the box. A board fell off, and heavily greased rifles and carbines slid to the concrete floor.

Both customs men scrambled into action, halting the loading and demanding to check everything already on board.

Sebastian felt better about his own nose. But what about those dogs? How could *they* have been so wrong? He touched the first dog's nose with his own. He sniffed. He touched the second dog's nose. The same. Their noses had been rubbed with vanilla extract. That was all they could smell. Just as all he had been able to smell was turpentine.

Maybe later he could figure out a way to let the customs men know what was wrong with their sniffing dogs. But for now he had something else to do. He left the customs men yelling for the loading to stop and calling for backup, and trotted on toward Berth 42, where the *Cleopatra* would be docking soon.

At the warehouse by Berth 42, there was a van parked. It said Karmine Kennels. Karmine—pronounced the same as Carmine? Was it Carmine Rothwinger? Was he just spelling his name differently to make it look better with Kennels? And what would his dogs be doing here?

Sebastian crept closer. He saw John and Hasan. They were talking to a man in a customs uniform. There was also a man in a brown uniform that said KARMINE KENNELS.

John reached down to pet one of the dogs, a German shepherd. "I don't understand, Roger. You use privately owned dogs for your sniffing?" John asked the customs man.

"Oh, no! They are our own handpicked dogs. And we do our own training, too," Roger answered. "But we house them in a privately owned kennel. That way they get all their immunization shots, feed, grooming, and housing cheaper than if we had to maintain our own—"

A dockside phone rang, and the customs man answered. "What? They didn't even sniff it out? You think maybe the dogs are sick or something? I don't know, but the Karmine guy's here right now. I'll try to find out what's going on."

Sebastian realized that Roger was hearing about the dogs at Berth 38. The man in the kennel uniform looked a little pale. He must have realized it, too. "I guess I'd better be going," he told John and Hasan. He trotted toward his van.

"Hold it!" Roger yelled at him. "I want to talk—"

The man broke into a run. "Catch him!" Roger shouted. Sebastian was about to go after him, but fortunately John and Hasan seemed to realize what was happening. John made a running leap and tackled the man, throwing him to the ground. By the time John had scrambled to his feet, Hasan was pulling the man toward the customs officer.

"I didn't do nothing!" the man yelled.

"Then why did you run?" John wanted to know. "If you haven't done anything, we'll know soon enough. And if you have, we'll know that, too. Now, what's all this about?" he asked Roger.

"I don't know what's going on, either," the customs man said, "but I'm sure going to find out. That was our man at Berth 38 I was talking to. He said his dogs didn't detect a load of weapons going out. They wouldn't ever have been discovered if some klutz of a longshoreman hadn't dropped one of the cases."

In his hiding place, Sebastian squared his jaw indignantly. Klutz! Were all humans alike? Did not one give him any credit? They wouldn't talk about him like that to his fuzzy face! He sighed. Yes, they would. They did it all the time.

"Somebody has tampered with those dogs—

maybe these dogs, too—and the only time they're out of our sight is when they're with Karmine Kennels," Roger said. "And judging from this fellow's reaction, I'd say that's where the answer is."

Hasan squatted down with his face near the dogs. He rubbed their ears and talked soothingly to them. Hasan leaned forward and sniffed. He wrinkled his nose. "Vanilla!" he said. "These dogs' noses have been rubbed with vanilla extract. When I was a child and we raised sheep, my father would rub the nose of a ewe with vanilla so she would accept an orphan lamb as her own. She thought that she and it smelled the same. It is an old farming trick."

The customs man shook his head, bewildered. "We'll begin a complete investigation, of course. If you will arrest this man on suspicion, that will keep him from warning whomever he's working for."

While they waited for a squad car with uniformed police to take the man back to the precinct, John read the man his rights. "You have the right to remain silent. You have the right to an attorney. . . . "

At least the man couldn't tell Rothwinger—if it *was* Rothwinger—that the police were on to his little game. But the cagey canine realized there was still work to be done.

"In the meantime, we're going to have to depend on ourselves to find your missing artifacts," the customs man said, echoing Sebastian's thoughts.

Not to worry. He, Sebastian (Super Sleuth), was on the job. And clues were beginning to fall into place. He was sure the business register would show that Karmine Kennels was only one of Carmine Rothwinger's businesses. There was Carmine Ship Lines, too. No wonder he got rich. He was smuggling things in and out and doctoring the dogs so they wouldn't detect anything illegal.

And Sebastian was sure he had another thing figured out, too. The culprit was Rothwinger—it had to be. Carmine Rothwinger had had all those replicas made of Egyptian artifacts. He had invited the public to look at them. People could easily testify that the pieces were fake. But Rothwinger had said that after satisfying the public's curiosity he was going to close his doors forever.

Sebastian was certain that Rothwinger was then going to substitute the real pieces for the fakes. He would be free to display and enjoy them without anyone ever being the least bit suspicious. Rothwinger was one of those eccentrics Hasan mentioned. But he had an extra helping of cunning!

His plan might have worked, too, had it not been for this detective. But Sebastian was getting ahead of himself, wasn't he? He still had to prove his theory. And he still had to find the stolen artifacts. A tad more difficult than theorizing, even for the four-on-the-floor furry detective.

7
All That Ends Well

By the time the patrol car had picked up the kennel man, the *Cleopatra* had arrived in port. Stealthily, Sebastian watched John and Hasan, armed with their warrant, board the *Cleopatra* for a search, as they had done with each docking ship. Slipping aboard in the confusion that followed, he observed the two of them upturning bunk mattresses, opening luggage, and thumping cabinets for hollow cavities that might secret the artifacts away.

For hours, they prodded, pushed, and pulled everything on the ship. They opened every box of dates; all they found were dates. They peered into every crate of olives; all they found were olives. And they thumped every barrel of olive oil to see if it thudded instead of sloshed. Nothing.

"They just aren't here," John said, obviously exasperated. "Let's hope we have more luck with the *Bastet*. It should be docked by now."

The three of them—John and Hasan in the open

and Sebastian skulking in the shadows of ware-houses—went to Berth 38, where the *Bastet* now stood, its boarding plank still up and customs officers lining the dock to be sure that no one left the ship.

John and Hasan went aboard and presented their search warrant to the captain, who shouted at them in a foreign language. Sebastian didn't understand, but he didn't need a translation to tell that the man was angry.

On board, they went through the same routine. They checked above and below decks. They even looked inside the smokestacks. Again, nothing.

How could he have been so wrong? Sebastian wondered.

"How could we have been so wrong?" John asked Hasan. "I felt sure we were on to something, especially after we found the dogs had been messed up for sniffing."

"I don't understand it, either, my friend John. I was positive that this Rothwinger was our man. Alas, nothing. I don't know what to do, except continue to search ships. I fear, though, we are too late."

Sebastian shed the overalls and cap and sat down on the dock's edge to think. He scratched a flea behind his left ear and watched idly as the fishing trawlers wove their way down the channel to their own docks.

Sea gulls dove and screamed at the trawlers, begging for a taste of their catch. And on board, the fishermen worked to sort their catches into the ice chests, ready for sale. Amusing how the little boats were all named, just as the big ships were.

I Sea U, *The Betsy Lou*, *Nefertiti*, *N Debt*—all of them paraded past. The men seemed to pay no attention at all to those noisy, pushy, diving birds.

Except for the *Nefertiti*, the birds were giving those boats a hard time. Wait a minute. Why weren't the birds diving at that boat? Its ice chests lined its deck, just as ice chests lined the other trawlers. Didn't they catch anything? *Nefertiti*—if memory served him right (and it always did)—was the name of an Egyptian queen. Egyptian! Of course, Carmine just couldn't resist, could he?

Sebastian made a dash for John—he had to get his attention. He yanked on John's pant leg, rumbling deep in his throat.

"Wha—" John nearly lost his balance. "Sebastian! You followed me, you naughty—"

Sebastian didn't wait. He ran along the dock, keeping pace with the *Nefertiti*. He could hear John behind him, yelling, "Come back, boy. Come, Sebastian." And he could hear Hasan right behind John, yelling, "What is it? What is going on?"

They'd find out soon enough, if they kept up with the old hairy hawkshaw. The trawler eased alongside a small pier, and the captain shut its motor down to a slow thrumming. Sebastian took a deep breath and made a dog's-width leap, landing with a thud on deck. A faint scent of gunpowder teased his nose. Was it from Hasan's spent bullets?

A man with a ship tattooed on his arm and holding a burlap bag tied at the top started yelling. Sebastian was sure the bag had at least a couple of the stolen artifacts in it. He bit into the bag and tugged. The man tugged back, kicking at Sebastian.

John jumped on board. Help at last! "Here, now," John yelled at him. "Let go of that bag, you naughty dog. I'm so sorry!"

Sebastian yanked back, growling, and the bag flew open, spilling dirty laundry all over the deck of the boat.

Startled, Sebastian let go. John tugged at his neck fur. "When I get you home, it's dry dog food for a week!" he scolded. "I'm so sorry," John told the man with the tattoo. "I just don't know what has come over him. I hope he didn't hurt anything."

The man snarled and gathered the clothes back into the bag. "Just get 'im away from here."

Subdued and embarrassed, Sebastian followed John onto the dock. He had been so sure this time. What about the sea gulls? They didn't seem to think the boat had any fish on board. Surely if they'd smelled fish, they'd have been diving at the boat.

And he'd been so sure he'd smelled gunpowder from spent bullets.

He plodded along the dock, sulking as John told him all the things that he wasn't going to get to do after this. He gave one last unhappy glance at the *Nefertiti*. The tattooed man and the one who'd been driving the boat were carrying an ice chest onto a truck that had backed up to the dock.

Wait a minute. *Both* of them carrying one ice chest? Hadn't the man yesterday carried one all by himself? And neither of these men looked like a weakling. There was only one thing that could make that chest as heavy as it seemed to be. And those ice chests were just big enough to hold bread boxes. They'd be perfect for hiding the artifacts. With one mighty jerk Sebastian freed himself from John's grasp. He dashed toward the *Nefertiti* with John and Hasan only footsteps behind. John was really angry this time. Sebastian had better be right!

With a great leap, Sebastian jumped against the tattooed man's shoulders. The man lost his balance, and both of them tumbled head first into the water.

Dog-paddling, Sebastian managed to propel himself to the dock, where Hasan pulled him out of the water. He shook vigorously, sending a rain of water over John, the boat pilot, and the open ice chest.

Sebastian pushed the chest onto its side. A box inside had broken open, and packing material spilled

out. A shiny brass bullet rolled from the packing and clattered onto the dock. There, looking back, was the golden head of a lion with turquoise inlays.

Hasan fished the tattooed man out of the water and handcuffed him. By that time John had handcuffed the other man. "You are both under arrest," John told them. "You have the right to remain silent. You . . ."

They stepped aboard the trawler and found the rest of the small artifacts in the other ice chests. The larger pieces were in the hold below decks.

John called for a patrol car to take the captain and the tattooed sailor to jail, where they just couldn't wait to tell the police that it was Carmine Rothwinger who had hired them to bring in the stolen artifacts. Rothwinger had known that the police would probably be watching the ships. So he'd sent out one of his fishing trawlers, the *Nefertiti*, to lay alongside the *Bastet* and take on the artifacts, which they then put into the ice chests.

Of course, Rothwinger hadn't counted on someone as clever as Sebastian. Just as the old crime hound had thought, Rothwinger had planned on substituting the real artifacts for his phony ones. He could have displayed them smugly, and after all the publicity about his phony ones, no one would have suspected the switch.

There were so many ways this case might have

gone awry. The thieves might have repacked the artifacts, discarding the spent bullets. And even if the artifacts had remained in their telltale cases (as they had), the dogs might have been tampered with (as they had been to allow an export out). Or the old super sleuth himself might have concentrated on the incoming ships, ignoring the small commercial and private boats that frequented the channel. Or the captain of the *Nefertiti* might have decided to go fishing while he was waiting for the contraband. In that case, his boat would have been just as fishy as the others, and the clever canine might never have noticed. There was an awful lot of luck involved in solving mysteries, Sebastian thought. Luck coupled with clever detection, that is.

Catching Rothwinger ended all his dirty dealings, smuggling arms out of the country, smuggling stolen goods in, and tampering with the customs dogs.

When Rothwinger and his helpers had been booked and jailed and photographs of the artifacts on the boat had been made for evidence, Hasan, with the help of the city museum, packed the precious treasures for their return. The boxes had first-class airline tickets—no cargo hold for them.

"I will miss you, my friend John—and my new friend, Sebastian," Hasan said before boarding. He scratched Sebastian's ear. *Mmmm*.

"Two days is much too short a visit, Hasan," John

said. "But I'm glad this case ended well. If it hadn't been for that klutzy longshoreman uncovering that box of weapons, and if Sebastian hadn't been so naughty and followed me, then jumped on that man and fallen overboard . . . "

"Ah, yes," Hasan said. "Such a lucky accident." He winked at Sebastian, chuckling.

Sebastian couldn't be sure, but he thought perhaps Hasan did understand. It was nice to think so, anyway.

He offered his paw to Hasan, who shook it quickly, then hurried to board his plane. He sniffed the air, testing the old nose. There was bubble gum nearby, raspberry flavor. And tobacco, a diet soda, and mustard. Mustard? If there was mustard, there must be a hamburger or a hot dog.

His nose led him to a gentleman who'd fallen asleep, probably waiting for his plane. The hot dog tilted dangerously near his tie.

Sebastian leaned close and slurped the hot dog down in one big gulp. It was the kind thing to do. Should he have let the man's tie get ruined?

"Sebastian!" John shouted. "Ready, boy?"

What kind of question was that? A super sleuth, especially a four-on-the-floor variety, was *always* ready for *anything*.